Fact Finders®

It's Back to School ... Way Back!

School in *the* CIVIL RIGHTS MOVEMENT

by Rachel A. Koestler-Grack

CAPSTONE PRESS
a capstone imprint

Fact Finder Books are published by Capstone Press,
1710 Roe Crest Drive, North Mankato, Minnesota 56003.
www.mycapstone.com

Library of Congress Cataloging-in-Publication Data
Names: Koestler-Grack, Rachel A., 1973–author.
Title: School in the civil rights movement / by Rachel A. Koestler-Grack.
Description: North Mankato, Minnesota: Capstone Press, an imprint of Capstone Press, [2017] |
Series: Fact finders. It's back to school ... way back! | Includes bibliographical references and
index.| Audience: Age 9-12. | Audience: Grades 4-6.
Identifiers: LCCN 2015048715| ISBN 9781515720997 (library binding) |
ISBN 9781515721031 (paperback) | ISBN 9781515721079 (ebook pdf)
Subjects: LCSH: Education—United States—History—20th century—Juvenile literature. |
Schools—United States—History—20th century—Juvenile literature. |
   Civil rights movements—United States—History—20th century—Juvenile literature.
Classification: LCC LA209.2 .K63 2017 | DDC 370.9730904—dc23
LC record available at http://lccn.loc.gov/2015048715

Editorial Credits
Editor: Nikki Potts
Designer: Kayla Rossow
Media Researcher: Jo Miller
Production Specialist: Kathy McColley

Photo Credits
Alamy: A.T. Willett, 27; Capstone Press: Gary Sundermeyer, 29; Corbis: AS400 DB, 17, Bettmann,
11, 14, 18; Getty Images: Michael Ochs Archives, 22, PhotoQuest, 20, Underwood Archives, 15;
Library of Congress Prints and Photographs, 26; Newscom: akg-images/Arthur Rothstein, 5,
Everett Collection, 7, 13, 19, 24, Frances M. Roberts, 28, Underwood Archives/UIG Universal
Images Group, cover; Shutterstock: Bartek Zyczynski, cover (background); Design Elements:
Shutterstock: Frank Rohde, iulias, marekuliasz, Undrey

Printed and bound in the USA.
009671F16

TABLE of CONTENTS

Chapter 1

STRUGGLING TOWARD EQUALITY

The history of African-Americans in the United States begins with slavery. In the 1600s slave traders began kidnapping Africans to bring them to North America as slaves. Slave traders sold most of the kidnapped Africans to plantation owners who depended on the slaves to work in their large fields.

Enslaved people led extremely difficult lives. Men, women, and children worked six days a week doing hard labor. Enslaved children began working around age 5 or 6. Plantation owners often broke up slave families. They sold some family members to other plantations. Slaves lived in crude cabins on the plantation.

Throughout the South and in some parts of the North, city officials built separate restaurants, shops, and theaters for African-Americans.

By the mid-1800s slavery was illegal in many northern states. Many slaves ran away from plantations and escaped to the North on the **Underground Railroad.** These safe routes ran from southern states to freedom in the northern states and Canada.

The North defeated the South in the Civil War (1861–1865) allowing all African-Americans to be free from slavery. But many whites still treated African-Americans poorly. Black people weren't allowed to eat next to white people in restaurants. They had to attend separate schools. They had separate bathrooms and drinking fountains. Many African-Americans lived in **segregated** areas that were often rundown and poorly kept.

Underground Railroad—system of helpful people and safe places for runaway slaves during the mid-1800s

segregate—to separate one racial group from another

The National Association for the Advancement of Colored People (NAACP) is devoted to gaining and protecting equal rights for African-Americans. In the 1950s the NAACP and others continued their work for **desegregation** and equal rights. This struggle for equality was called the civil rights movement.

People of all races worked for civil rights. Many of the civil rights activists participated in marches, **boycotts,** and sit-ins. Demonstrations were a peaceful way of showing that African-Americans wanted and deserved equality.

Much violence took place during the civil rights movement. Many African-Americans and civil rights activists were killed in mob attacks and **lynchings.** One hate group was called the Ku Klux Klan (KKK). They believed they had the right to hang the accused without a fair trial. They often went unpunished.

desegregation—getting rid of any laws or practices that separate people of different races
boycott—to refuse to buy or use a product of service to protest something believed to be wrong or unfair
lynching—putting to death, often by handing, by mob action and without legal authority

Many people participated in the civil rights movement. They worked for changes in government laws. The changes included school desegregation, the Civil Rights Act of 1964, and the Voting Rights Act of 1965.

African-Americans participate in a sit-in at a whites-only lunch counter in Nashville, Tennessee, in 1960.

FACT

In 1960 the U.S. Supreme Court ruled that blacks didn't have to sit in separate sections of trains, buses, and planes. To test the new ruling civil rights activists traveled throughout the South on what were called Freedom Rides. Mobs often attacked the Freedom Riders and many people were injured.

EVENTS DURING THE CIVIL RIGHTS MOVEMENT

1954

In a series of cases called Brown v. Board of Education, Topeka, the Supreme Court outlaws segregation in public schools.

1955

The Montgomery bus boycott begins on December 5, 1955, and ends on December 21, 1956, when the Supreme Court orders Montgomery to integrate its bus system.

Fourteen-year-old Emmett Till is murdered in Money, Mississippi, for supposedly whistling at a white woman.

1956

Bus boycotts begin in Birmingham and Mobile, Alabama, and in Tallahassee, Florida.

1957

The Little Rock Nine attend Central High School in Little Rock, Arkansas. These students are escorted between classes by federal troops for protection from white students.

David Richmond, Franklin McCain, Joseph McNeil, and Ezell Blair Jr. stage a sit-in at the F. W. Woolworth's store in Greensboro, North Carolina, when they are refused service. This incident inspired other sit-ins throughout the South.

1960

Ruby Bridges becomes the first African-American student to attend an all-white elementary school in New Orleans, Louisiana.

1961

Freedom Rides move throughout the southeastern United States.

Freedom Riders are attacked by whites at a bus terminal in Anniston, Alabama.

1963

More than 250,000 activists gather for the March on Washington, the largest civil rights demonstration in Washington, D.C.'s history.

Four girls die when the KKK bombs the Sixteenth Street Baptist Church in Birmingham, Alabama.

Martin Luther King Jr. leads a march for civil rights from Selma, Alabama, to Montgomery, Alabama.

1965

The Voting Rights Act is passed, putting an end to all methods used by states to keep African-Americans from voting.

Washington, D.C.

WEST VIRGINIA

KENTUCKY

VIRGINIA

Nashville

TENNESSEE

Greensboro

NORTH CAROLINA

1 Jailed

Charlotte
Rock Hill

ARKANSAS

9 Arrested & Released

2 Arrested & Released

Winnsboro

Little Rock

Anniston

SOUTH CAROLINA

Money

Birmingham

Jackson

Selma

GEORGIA

MISSISSIPPI

306 Jailed

Montgomery

ALABAMA

LOUISIANA

Tallahassee

FLORIDA

	May 14, 1961 Freedom Ride
	May 17, 1961 Freedom Ride
	Selma to Montgomery March
●	cities of major events
✳	violence

Chapter 2

SEGREGATED SCHOOLS

In the 1950s most U.S. schools were segregated. Many felt white children and African-American children should not attend the same schools.

In cities African-American students attended their own public schools. The schools had indoor plumbing and electricity. But many of the schools were run down and in need of repairs.

In rural areas African-Americans often attended classes in abandoned cabins, barns, and churches. Many rural schools were one-room buildings with shaky floors. They had only a potbellied stove for heat. In many cases the only way for an African-American community to construct a new building was to close the school for several months and use the teacher's salary to pay for building supplies.

African-American schools were in constant risk of being **vandalized**. Hate groups such as the KKK sometimes set fire to African-American schools. Some African-American families organized secret schools in rural areas to keep students safe. They also held classes on different days of the week or in different buildings each week.

White children and adults sometimes **harassed** black students on their way to school. The sight of African-American students carrying books angered some whites. They did not believe African-Americans deserved an education.

A teacher reads to his students at a segregated school in Uno, Virginia, on February 2, 1947.

vandalize—to needlessly damage property
harass—to bother or annoy again and again

The NAACP fought for school **integration.** In the 1950s the NAACP took a series of cases to the U.S. Supreme Court. The cases were combined in Brown v. Board of Education. Linda Brown was a 7-year-old student who lived in Topeka, Kansas. She had to travel across town to attend an African-American school. NAACP attorneys argued that forcing students to attend separate schools because of race harmed African-American children.

In 1954 the Supreme Court ruled in favor of the NAACP. Until then segregation had been allowed under a practice known as "separate but equal." The thinking was that if a separate park, school, or hospital for blacks was just as good as a park, school, or hospital for whites, then it was OK. In reality the **institutions** for blacks were never as good. NAACP attorneys argued that separate was not equal—and the Supreme Court agreed. The Court forced schools to integrate.

integration—the act or practice of making schools and other places open to people of all races

institution—a large organization where people live or work together

The U.S. Military escorts the Little Rock Nine as they leave Central High School in Arkansas.

Many people still opposed integrated schools. In 1957 nine black students tried to attend Central High School in Little Rock, Arkansas. But state officials did not let them into the building. The U.S. government sent federal troops to protect the students from angry white students and parents. Troops escorted the Little Rock Nine into school. They also walked with them between classes.

Some African-Americans dropped out of white schools because they did not want to be harassed. Some parents took their children out of schools because angry whites threatened the students' lives. But most African-American students remained in integrated schools. Many white children were unsure of how to act toward black students. They were not used to attending racially mixed schools. Some white children were afraid to include African-American students in games. They were afraid to choose them as partners in class projects because they did not want to be harassed themselves. But many white children showed courage by making friends with African-American students.

Ruby Bridges

In 1960 6-year-old Ruby Bridges became the first African-American student to attend a desegregated elementary school. A federal court ordered William Frantz Elementary School in New Orleans to allow both African-American students and white students to attend. On her first day of classes many people protested outside the school. Ruby and her mother spent the entire day in the principal's office because of the protestors.

Many parents pulled their children out of school for the entire year. On her second day, Ruby thought she was early when she arrived to an empty classroom. Ruby was the only student in her class that year. But she went to school every day. Because of Ruby's courage, more African-American children attended William Frantz Elementary School the next year.

Federal marshals escort Ruby Bridges into William Frantz Public School during her second week of school.

Chapter 3

A LIMITED EDUCATION

Integration in schools did not come quickly. Many schools remained segregated for several years before federal courts forced them to enroll African-American students.

In the 1950s most African-American schools taught job skills in addition to basic subjects. Schools offered classes in agriculture, cooking, sewing, carpentry, and other trades. Some states did not allow African-American schools to offer classes that prepared students for college. They were not allowed to offer such classes as Latin and advanced mathematics.

Both African-Americans and whites paid taxes. But most tax dollars for education went to white schools. Most African-American schools did not have enough money for sports activities, school libraries, or music programs.

School busing was not always available for African-American students. Children often walked several miles to get to school. Other students rode to school on city buses. Segregation laws forced African-Americans to ride in the back of city buses.

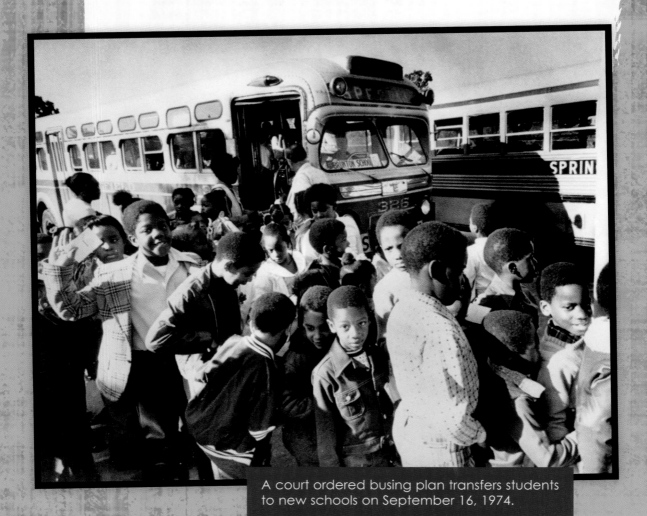

A court ordered busing plan transfers students to new schools on September 16, 1974.

In the South there were often more African-American students than white students. But there were fewer schools. Two sessions of classes were sometimes held to allow all children to attend.

Teachers in African-American schools had limited funds to spend on teaching materials. Teachers learned to be creative with their teaching methods. Many used a baseball instead of a globe to show the motion of Earth. In geography lessons they spread sand on the floor to make a relief map. Many teachers used the Bible and the Farmer's Almanac to teach children how to read.

A teacher addresses students at recently integrated Bethune Elementary School.

An African-American student reads during a school day at her integrated Boston school in September 1965.

In the 1950s schools used primers to teach children how to read. Primers taught children **moral** and patriotic values. They promoted faithfulness to employers and respect for authority. Primers portrayed the United States as a land of equal opportunity. But African-Americans did not have equal opportunities. Primers also taught that hard work and honesty brought success. But many employers did not hire or respect African-Americans. The books taught about the Pilgrims, the Puritans, and America's Founding Fathers. But books did not include lessons on African-American history. Primers supported the way whites thought and acted but often portrayed African-Americans as uncivilized, thoughtless, and unintelligent.

moral—belief about what is right and wrong

Chapter 4

STUDENTS AS ACTIVISTS

Many African-American children were active in the civil rights movement. They spent their summers helping civil rights organizations. Some high school students dropped out to become full-time activists. Many participated in demonstrations, marches, boycotts, and sit-ins.

Mary McLeod Bethune

Mary McLeod Bethune

Mary McLeod Bethune was a trail-blazing educator. She was born in 1875 in Mayesville, South Carolina. Mary worked hard doing chores to help her family. She sometimes worked as many as 10 hours a day on the farm.

When Mary was 7 years old she began attending a **mission school**. She walked five miles to school each day. After Mary graduated from mission school at age 10, she went to an African-American girls boarding school in North Carolina. In order to pay for her room and board, she cleaned and did laundry at the school.

In 1896 Bethune began teaching in the South. In 1904 she opened the Daytona Normal and Industrial Institute for Negro Girls in Florida. The first year there were only five students. The school eventually became Bethune-Cookman University. Bethune served as the school president from 1904 to 1942, and again in 1946 and 1947.

Bethune was active in the civil rights movement. She served as the director of Negro Affairs of the federal National Youth Administration. She worked with President Franklin Delano Roosevelt on **minority** issues and served as vice president of the NAACP.

mission school—a school for the religious instruction of children

minority—group of people different from the larger group of which it is a part because of race, religion, politics, or nationality

African-American children are sprayed with water and attacked by dogs during a protest in May 1963.

Children helped bring national attention to the civil rights movement. In 1951 Barbara Rose Johns demanded improvements at her high school in Farmville, Virginia. Barbara persuaded her classmates to join in a boycott against Morton High School. The NAACP represented her case in court.

In 1955 police arrested 15-year-old Claudette Colvin. She refused to give up her seat on a city bus for a white woman. Nine months later the Montgomery bus boycott began. People hoped that the loss of fares would force the city to integrate its transportation. During the boycott children walked to school instead of taking city buses. The boycott lasted for 382 days, until the U.S. Supreme Court outlawed segregation in Montgomery.

In May 1963 more than 1,000 students were arrested and jailed for demonstrating against segregation in Birmingham, Alabama. Many adults had already been jailed. Civil rights leaders asked everyone, including children, to protest. Some of the protestors were only 6 years old. Police unleashed police dogs on the protestors. Firefighters sprayed them with water from high-pressure fire hoses.

Many young African-Americans also participated in sit-ins. During sit-ins activists sat in the whites-only sections of segregated restaurants. Workers refused to serve African-Americans who sat in the white section. Activists did not give up their seats when they were asked to move. Many activists were arrested during sit-ins.

Some children were hurt or killed during the civil rights movement. In 1955 14-year-old Emmett Till was brutally murdered. He was said to have whistled at a white woman. The KKK and other groups also bombed homes, schools, and churches.

FACT

On September 15, 1963, a bomb set by KKK members killed four African-American girls at the Sixteenth Street Baptist Church in Birmingham, Alabama. The victims were 14-year-olds Cynthia Wesley, Carole Robertson, and Addie Mae Collins and 11-year-old Denise McNair.

Chapter 5

CELEBRATIONS FOR STRENGTH

Church groups gave many people hope during the civil rights movement. Many victories were celebrated in church. People met there to discuss local boycotts, marches, and sit-ins. They shared news and information with each other. Leaders such as Reverend Martin Luther King Jr. taught people to be patient and strong. They encouraged civil rights activists to be nonviolent in their fight for equality.

Members of the First Baptist Church of Montgomery, Alabama, cheer for civil rights leaders during the bus boycott in 1956.

Martin Luther King established the Southern Christian Leadership Conference (SCLC) in 1957. The organization worked to gain full equality for African-Americans. SCLC held leadership training programs, citizen education projects, and voter registration drives.

African-Americans sang **spirituals** during church services. They sang these songs to encourage and inspire each other. Most spirituals were based on Biblical stories about people being saved from suffering. Spirituals gave people strength to make it through difficult times.

Activists also sang freedom songs during civil rights meetings, marches, and demonstrations. The songs gave activists encouragement and hope. They sang songs such as "Freedom Now," "We Shall Overcome," and "Woke Up This Morning with Freedom on My Mind."

spiritual—religious folk song originated by African-Americans in the South

On January 1, 1863, President Abraham Lincoln gave a speech called the Emancipation Proclamation. He declared slaves free in southern states that were not already under Union control. After the Civil War (1861–1865), many African-Americans began celebrating Emancipation Day on January 1.

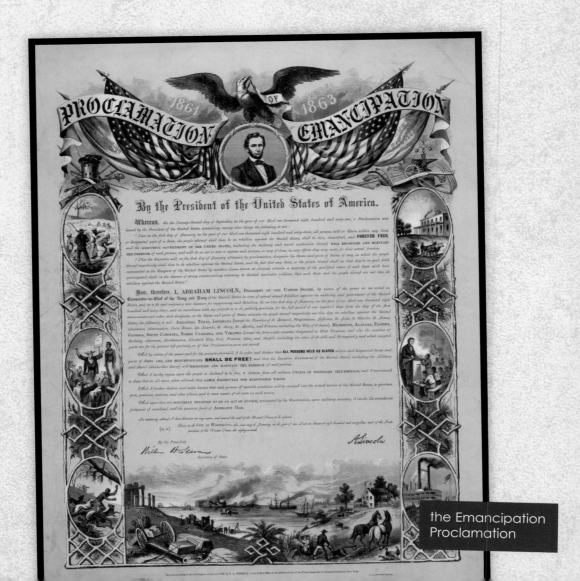

the Emancipation Proclamation

Gospel singers perform at a Junteenth celebration in Tucson, Arizona in 1985.

People in the southwestern United States celebrated Emancipation Day on June 19. On this day in 1865, news reached Texas that the Union had won the Civil War and that all slaves were free. African-Americans also called this celebration Juneteenth.

During Juneteenth people dressed in fancy clothing. In the mid-1800s laws regulated how slaves dressed. Enslaved people had not been allowed to wear fancy or expensive clothing. Today Juneteenth is celebrated with parades, carnivals, picnics, and church services.

Today, U.S. schools honor civil rights leader Martin Luther King Jr. People celebrate Martin Luther King Jr. Day on the third Monday in January. Schools close for this national holiday. Between 1950 and 1970, the NAACP and workers in the civil rights movement brought about many changes in U.S. laws. Many men, women, and children joined together to fight for their rights. Their dedication helped end segregation in schools, transportation, and other public places. Congress also passed many laws to protect the civil rights of all U.S. citizens.

A student from Manhattan Country School holds a sign honoring Martin Luther King Jr. during the 21st Annual Martin Luther King Jr. Commemorative Walk in New York.

MAKE A GLOBE

African-American schools did not receive as much funding as white schools. Teachers often made their own school supplies.

What You Need

newspaper

large bowl

1 cup flour

2 cups water

wooden spoon

6-inch diameter foam ball, available at craft stores

green and blue craft paints

paintbrushes of various sizes

map of the world or globe

foam plate

permanent marker

wooden or bamboo skewers

6-inch foam disc

What You Do

1. Rip several sheets of newspaper into 2-inch strips.

2. In a large bowl, combine flour and water. Stir until well mixed.

3. Dip a strip of newspaper into the flour-water mixture. Make sure the paper is well-coated.

4. Wrap the paper around the foam ball.

5. Repeat steps 3 and 4 until the ball is completely covered with paper. Let the ball dry overnight.

6. When the ball is dry, paint it blue. Set the ball on a foam plate while painting it. Let the paint dry. Looking at a map or globe, paint the continents onto the ball in green. Let the paint dry. Use the permanent marker to label the continents and oceans.

7. Carefully push the wooden skewer into the bottom of the globe. You may need to use two skewers to firmly support the globe.

8. Push the other ends of the skewers into the foam disc, which is the base.

GLOSSARY

boycott (BOI-kot)—to refuse to buy or use a product of service to protest something believed to be wrong or unfair

desegregation (dee-seg-ruh-GAY-shuhn)—getting rid of any laws or practices that separate people of different races

harass (ha-RASS)—to bother or annoy again and again

institution (in-sti-TOO-shuhn)—a large organization where people live or work together

integration (in-tuh-GRAY-shuhn)—the act or practice of making schools and other places open to people of all races

lynching (LINCH-ing)—putting to death, often by handing, by mob action and without legal authority

minority (muh-NOR-i-tee)—group of people different from the larger group of which it is a part because of race, religion, politics, or nationality

mission school (MISH-uhn SKOOL)—group of people different from the larger group of which it is a part because of race, religion, politics, or nationality

moral (MOR-uhls)—belief about what is right and wrong

segregate (SEG-ruh-gate)—to separate one racial group from another

spiritual (SPIHR-uh-choo-uhl)—religious folk song originated by African-Americans in the South

Underground Railroad (UHN-dur-ground RAYL-rohd)—system of helpful people and safe places for runaway slaves during the mid-1800s

vandalize (VAN-duhl-ize)—to needlessly damage property

READ MORE

deRubertis, Barbara. *Let's Celebrate Martin Luther King Jr. Day.* Holidays & Heroes. New York: The Kane Press, 2013.

Feinstein, Stephen. *Inspiring African-American Civil Rights Leaders.* African-American Collective Biographies. Berkeley Heights, N.J.: Enslow Publishers, 2013.

Mortensen, Lori. *Voices of the Civil Rights Movement: A Primary Source Exploration of the Struggle for Racial Equality.* We Shall Overcome. North Mankato, Minn.: Capstone Press, 2015.

INTERNET SITES

FactHound offers a safe, fun way to find Internet sites related to this book. All of the sites on FactHound have been researched by our staff.

Here's all you do:

Visit *www.facthound.com*

Type in this code: 9781515720997

Super-cool stuff!

Check out projects, games and lots more at
www.capstonekids.com

CRITICAL THINKING USING THE COMMON CORE

1. Many civil rights activists, including children, participated in sit-ins during the civil rights movement. What is a sit-in? Describe a famous sit-in event. (Key Ideas and Details)

2. Take a look at the map on page 9. Then match each event to the location on the map. (Craft and Structure)

3. What types of subjects were African-American children taught at school? How do their classes differ from the subjects you learn today? (Key Ideas and Details)

INDEX